The World Needs Beautiful Things

In honor of my grandparents Rabbi Albert and Leah Binder Silverman, Anne Berkowitz, and Charlie, the original Bezalel

—L.R.B.

To my beloved family, Alice and Enrico Jeremiah

—D.F.

KAR-BEN PUBLISHING, INC.
A division of Lerner Publishing Group, Inc.
241 First Avenue North
Minneapolis, MN 55401 USA
1-800-4-KARBEN

Website address: www.karben.com

Main body text set in Adrianna regular 16/24.
Typeface provided by Chank.

Library of Congress Cataloging-in-Publication Data
Names: Berkowitz, Leah Rachel, 1981- author. | Fabbri, Daniele, illustrator.
Title: The world needs beautiful things : the story of Bezalel the collector / by Leah Rachel Berkowitz ; illustrated by Daniele Fabbri.
Description: Minneapolis : Kar-Ben Publishing, [2018] | Series: Bible | Summary: Despite his parents' and friends' objections, Bezalel collects beautiful things, such as shiny stones and colored string, while a slave in Egypt and during the Exodus, which pleases God.
Identifiers: LCCN 2017030086| ISBN 9781512444483 (lb) | ISBN 9781512444490 (pb) | ISBN 9781541524019 (eb pdf)
Subjects: LCSH: Bezalel (Biblical figure)--Juvenile fiction. | CYAC: Bezalel (Biblical figure)—Fiction. | Collectors and collecting—Fiction. | Jews—History—To 1200 B.C.—Fiction. | Egypt—History—New Kingdom, ca. 1550-ca. 1070 B.C.—Fiction.
Classification: LCC PZ7.1.B4576 Wor 2018 | DDC [E]—dc23

LC record available at https://lccn.loc.gov/2017030086

Manufactured in the United States of America
1-42517-26194-10/25/2017

The World Needs Beautiful Things

Leah Rachel Berkowitz
illustrated by Daniele Fabbri

KAR-BEN
PUBLISHING

From the time he was a little boy, Bezalel loved to collect things. His eyes were drawn to shiny stones, colored strings, and even a bug if it had shiny, shimmering green wings.

Bezalel brought each treasure home to his Beautiful Things Box.

Bezalel and the rest of the Israelites were slaves in Egypt. The taskmasters grew angry when Bezalel dropped bricks into the mud to pick up a scaly piece of skin shed by a snake.

"Stop that!" his friends shouted. "You'll get us in trouble!
Besides, you don't need all those stones, strings, and bug wings."
Bezalel just smiled. "Each of these things is beautiful in its
own way, and the world needs beautiful things."

Bezalel never stopped searching for beauty and color.
When his life felt gray, he took out his Beautiful Things Box.
He pressed smooth stones to his cheek and wrapped
colorful strings around his fingers, forgetting for a
moment that he was a slave.

One day, Bezalel heard amazing news. Pharaoh was allowing the slaves to go free!
But they would have to leave Egypt immediately. The Israelites hurried to pack for their journey.

Bezalel's parents begged him to leave the Beautiful Things Box behind. "We can only take what we can carry," said his father.

"And what we absolutely need," said his mother. "You don't need all those stones, strings, and bug wings."

But Bezalel insisted, "Each of these things is beautiful in its own way, and the world needs beautiful things." Bezalel took his Beautiful Things Box and walked with the Israelites to freedom.

Bezalel saw many beautiful things as the Israelites
left Egypt: the bright full moon lighting their path . . .

... walls of water on either side of them
as they crossed the Red Sea ...

. . . pillars of fire and cloud that guided them
on their journey.
  These things were too big for the
Beautiful Things Box, so Bezalel tried to
collect them in his mind.

He also found many things that he *could* put in his Beautiful Things Box.

"Stop grabbing things out of the sand!" moaned his parents. "You don't need more stones, strings, or bug wings."

But Bezalel gripped his Beautiful Things Box and kept walking.

One day, God called to Moses, the leader of the Israelites. "I want you to build a *mishkan*—a place for Me to dwell when I visit the Israelites," God told Moses. "It will be like a beautiful room in your house for a special guest."

Moses was flustered. "Where are we supposed to find what we need to build Your house, God? We left Egypt with nothing, and we're in the middle of the desert!"

"The Israelites can bring Me gifts," God said. "Gold, silver, and copper. Strings of blue, purple, and red. Wood, oil, and spices."

"What if they don't have anything beautiful?" Moses asked.

"Everyone can find something," God promised, "if they know where to look."

The Israelites surrounded Moses as he came down the mountain. "What does God want?" they asked.

"God wants us to build a house out of beautiful things," said Moses.

There was silence. How could they build a house for God with only what they had carried out of Egypt?

"God suggested string. Does anybody have string to help us get started?" asked Moses doubtfully.

"I have string!" said a small voice.
Everyone turned to look as Bezalel stepped
forward, clutching his Beautiful Things Box. "I have
red, blue, and purple. What color does God want?"

The Israelites' mouths hung open as
Bezalel spread his treasures on the ground.
"I remember seeing trees with white
flowers on the other side of the mountain,"
Bezalel added. "Their trunks might be good
for building. I saw twisty olive trees too!"

Then something strange happened. The Israelites began to see blossoms poking out of the prickly cacti, and the twisty olive trees at the feet of forbidding mountains. They started their own Beautiful Things Boxes and brought them to Bezalel.

Moses ran to tell God. "You were right!
We've found many beautiful things!"

God looked at Bezalel, who was arranging stones by color and shape. "Bezalel!" said God. "You will design the mishkan!"

Bezalel's heart pounded. "Me?"

"Yes!" said God. "You love beautiful things. You found them in Egypt. You found them in the desert. You will build My dwelling place. Because . . . I love beautiful things too!"

So Bezalel described the beautiful images he saw in his mind, and together he and the other Israelites sketched his plans in the sand.

Then they started building with the materials they'd collected—wood from the desert trees, animal skins dyed bright colors, and bits of metal from rings and belt buckles.

And when the structure was complete, they wove tapestries, made lamps, crushed olives for oil, and mixed spices for incense.

Bezalel smiled at the finished mishkan. "This is the biggest Beautiful Things Box ever," he said. "Now every time God visits, there will be a beautiful place for God to dwell."

Author's Note

Bezalel appears in the biblical book of Exodus, where he is chosen by God to design and build the *mishkan*, God's dwelling place among the Israelites. The Torah tells us that God gave Bezalel skills in every type of craft, working with stone, wood, and metal. The other Israelites helped, too, bringing so many gifts that Moses eventually had to tell them to stop!

Bezalel's name means "in God's shadow," and it reminds us of a phrase in Genesis: "*B'tzelem Elohim* (in the image of God) God created human beings." Bezalel's name can help us remember that everyone is a reflection of God, even those who look different or act differently from others.